With love to our little angel, Zach
~ Mimi

THE WISE ANIMAL HANDBOOK

Kate B. Jerome

ARCADIA KIDS

Attempt
new
skills
from
time
.to
time.

Just **try** to think them **through.**

And if you **find** you're left **behind...**

...then change your point of view.

Try not to think of just yourself.

Invent new ways to share.

Stay close to friends whom you can trust.

But
always
be
aware.

Avoid the tattle in the tale.

Insist that **truth** is **best.**

Embrace with pride the strengths you have.

Demand
to be
impressed.

Enjoy the **peace** that **nature** brings.

Ignore what's just for show.

Join **forces** when the road gets **rough.**

Admit
when you
don't know.

Remember **family** is the **best.**

Despite the **ups** and **downs.**

Don't **hide** from things that you must **face.**

Make
joyful
laughing
sounds.

Eat **healthy** food to **grow** up **strong.**

Be **patient** with your **friends.**

Try not to take a stubborn stand.

Be
quick
to make
amends.

Excuse yourself when manners slip.

Be **helpful** every **day**.

Keep **trying** **hard.** even when it's

But
don't
forget to
play!

And **sing**

...and **dance** each **day!**

Written by Kate B. Jerome
Design and Production: Lumina Datamatics, Inc.
Coloring Illustrations: Tom Pounders
Research: Eric Nyquist

Cover Images: See back cover

Interior Images: 002 Anetapics/Shutterstock.com; 003 George Green/Shutterstock.com; 004 Sergey Uryadnikov/Shutterstock.com; 005 Gnomeandi/Shutterstock.com; 006 Bruce MacQueen/Shutterstock.com; 007 Henk Bentlage/Shutterstock.com; 008 M.M./Shutterstock.com; 009 Mikael Damkier/Shutterstock.com; 010 Brendan van Son/Shutterstock.com; 011 Michael Pettigrew/Shutterstock.com; 012 StevenRussellSmithPhotos/Shutterstock.com; 013 Pakhnyushchy/Shutterstock.com; 014 Patjo/Shutterstock.com; 015 Quinn Martin/Shutterstock.com; 016 Lincoln Rogers/Shutterstock.com; 017 Dirk Ercken/Shutterstock.com; 018 Karel Gallas/Shutterstock.com; 019 Orangecrush/Shutterstock.com; 020 Guenter-foto/Shutterstock.com; 021 Janecat/Shutterstock.com; 022 Shironina/Shutterstock.com; 023 Annette Shaff/Shutterstock.com; 024 Vitaly Titov/Shutterstock.com; 025 Rohappy/Shutterstock.com; 026 MattiaATH/Shutterstock.com; 027 Otsphoto/Shutterstock.com; 028 FikMik/Shutterstock.com; 029 Four Oaks/Shutterstock.com; 030 Ekaterina Kolomeets/Shutterstock.com; 031 Hugh Lansdown/Shutterstock.com.

Published by Arcadia Kids, a division of Arcadia Publishing and
The History Press, Charleston, SC

For all general information contact Arcadia Publishing at:
Telephone: 843-853-2070
Email: sales@arcadiapublishing.com

For Customer Service and Orders:
Toll Free: 1-888-313-2665
Visit us on the Internet at www.arcadiapublishing.com

Library of Congress Cataloging-in-Publication data is on file with the publisher.

Printed in China

Arkansas State **Insect**

Honeybee

Read Together

The honeybee was named the state insect in 1973. Lawmakers felt the bee was like the people of Arkansas with its hardworking spirit.

Arkansas State Mammal

White-tailed Deer

Read Together The white-tailed deer was named the state mammal in 1993. There are about one million deer in the state of Arkansas!